D0356724

WATCH
OUT

WATCH OUT

Alison Hughes

orca soundings

ORCA BOOK PUBLISHERS

Library and Archives Canada Cataloguing in Publication

Title: Watch out / Alison Hughes.
Names: Hughes, Alison, 1966– author.
Series: Orca soundings.

Description: Series statement: Orca soundings

Identifiers: Canadiana (print) 20190066326 |
Canadiana (ebook) 20190066350 | ISBN 9781459822351 (softcover) |
ISBN 9781459822368 (PDF) | ISBN 9781459822375 (EPUB)

Classification: LCC PS8615.U3165 W38 2019 | DDC jc813/.6—dc23

Library of Congress Control Number: 2019934064
Simultaneously published in Canada and the United States in 2019

Summary: In this high-interest novel for teens, fifteen-year-old
Charlie investigates a series of break-ins in his neighborhood.

*Orca Book Publishers is committed to reducing the consumption
of nonrenewable resources in the making of our books. We make
every effort to use materials that support a sustainable future.*

Orca Book Publishers gratefully acknowledges the support for its
publishing programs provided by the following agencies: the Government of
Canada, the Canada Council for the Arts and the Province of British Columbia
through the BC Arts Council and the Book Publishing Tax Credit.

Edited by Tanya Trafford
Cover images by Stocksy.com/Marcel (front) and
Shutterstock.com/Krasovski Dmitri (back)

ORCA BOOK PUBLISHERS
orcabook.com

Printed and bound in Canada.

22 21 20 19 • 4 3 2 1

For Maureen

Chapter One

"Doorbell," said Tom. My brother didn't even look up from his computer.

"Oh, man!" I had *just* poured both of us bowls of cereal. I had *just* rushed them upstairs, spoons shoved in my back pocket. I was rushing because cereal needs to be eaten within thirty seconds of pouring in the milk, of course. For prime cereal/milk blending. Anybody knows that. Leave it one or two minutes and that cereal is doomed. It turns into a mucky, soggy mess. And who wants to eat that?

The doorbell rang again.

"Charlie! *Doorbell*." I was busy choking back a few bites of perfect cereal. Tom grabbed one of his crutches and poked me with it. "C'mon. Go see who it is."

Last week Tom broke his leg in two places in one of the most spectacular injuries in the history of Walter Watts High School's football team. (The Wildcats. Name another *W* animal. Okay, I just thought of wolves, which would have been way better. Also wolverines. Never mind.) Anyway, it was a really grim injury. A hall-of-famer.

Even the doctor called it a "super-ugly, ugly break." You know when a *doctor* looks scared and says "ugly" twice that it's a bad one. It was one of those injuries they play over and over and over on the sports roundups. You know the ones—a baseball player crashing into the wall trying to make the catch, or a ref accidentally getting clocked by a giant linebacker. Maybe with a voice-over of the announcer saying, "*Oh!* That's gotta hurt!"

It was brutal, but it made Tom a minor celebrity at school. Who knew that a crippling injury was a ticket to popularity? I didn't. I might have to try it some time. It wasn't as if Tom needed more attention. Tall, popular, athletic— Tom was one of those twelfth-graders we tenth-graders pretty much hate. Well, not *hate*. He's my brother, so that's the wrong word. Resent? No, that's too negative. Envy? Bingo.

But I did feel bad for him when he got injured. It was the kind of injury where parents run onto the field. The kind of injury where a leg bends in several places that no leg should.

The kind of injury where *bone* rips right through the skin (I'm feeling sick just thinking about it). The kind of injury where everybody holds their hands over their mouths. Or sucks in their lips and groans or says, *Jeez.* Or just turns away and prays that people with stronger stomachs will deal with it. I was in that last group. Mom was the parent running onto the field. And Uncle Dave too. Not a parent, but an adult. Sort of.

Now Tom was stuck in a huge cast. A toe-to-hip cast. What a massive hassle! For me especially. Because Tom was going to be, as far as I could see, living a great life for the next few months. Sure, he was in a bit of pain. Okay, a lot of pain. But he had medicine to help control that. He had special permission from school to do his schoolwork from home for a few weeks. He had his computer and his books. And he had a 24/7 personal servant. Me.

Uncle Dave had piggybacked him up to our room after he got back from the hospital. And other than some slow crutching to the bathroom, that's where he's been. Watching Netflix, playing video games, making music on his computer.

So I had to pick up the slack around the house. Do everything. Well, everything other than make the money. Mom took care of that one. She had a job cleaning the operating rooms at the hospital. She didn't panic much at all about Tom's leg once she knew he was okay. She's seen enough gore, I guess. She knows things heal. She's a tough cookie, as Uncle Dave says.

So Tom's injury became my problem. Mom works, and Uncle Dave, who is currently living in our basement, is looking for work. In theory. He also does volunteer stuff and other various things. That means I had to do all the yard work. Garbage. All the housework. All the running food upstairs, all the taking dirty dishes downstairs. All the stacking dirty dishes in the dishwasher. All the unwrapping and cooking of frozen foods. Everything.

Including answering doorbells.

I pounded down the stairs and gave the peephole a quick glance. But I knew who it would be. It was the middle of the day. I yanked open the door on the third ring. Gary is our mail carrier. No matter the weather, Gary always seems to have a cold. His baseball hat is too big for his little head. His mail bag looks too heavy for him to carry. It practically hangs to his knees.

"Another package for ya," Gary said to the front step.

Gary always looks at something else when he is talking to you. At first I found this confusing. For example, he'd tell our mailbox it was going to rain.

Or mention to his shoes that postage rates were going up. But now I know he's actually talking to me. He's not so into eye contact. He's just an oddball, Mom says.

Gary wiped his nose with the back of his hand as he shoved the package at me. "For Tom, actually."

"Thanks, Gary," I said. This is where the door should be shutting, right? Mail guy comes with package. Mail guy delivers package. It's done. That's how normal mail people do things. But not Gary.

"Amazon again," he said, pointing to the package.

"Yep. Sure is." I gritted my teeth and tried to be nice. Gary obviously didn't have much of a life. He always wanted to stop and talk, even if it was only about mail. Or the weather. Or…actually, that was it. Mail and weather. Those were the only things we ever talked about.

"You guys sure get lots of packages," said Gary.

I sagged against the doorframe. Gary is a death-by-boredom kind of guy. I was really, really hoping he wasn't going to tell me yet again how packages are tracked before they're delivered. That one was a long, painful ramble.

"Yep, we sure do. My brother does, actually."

"Yeah? What did he order?" He said this to the porch. He didn't care. He was just making lame conversation.

But somehow I hate it when he flat-out asks what is in the packages. It isn't like there is ever anything exciting or private in them. Just electronic equipment and software for the music Tom makes on his computer.

It is the principle of the thing. Gary just shouldn't ask. Isn't that against some mail-carrier code? Aren't they just supposed to silently deliver things through rain and hail? This was like a grocery clerk asking why you bought that broccoli or how you were going to cook it. Mail, like broccoli, just seems private to me.

I don't know. Maybe I'm the one with the problem.

"Oh, just stuff. You know. Brrr…it's a little chilly."

Gary showed no sign of moving off the step. The guy could not take a hint. Ever.

He lifted his cap and scratched his mop of red hair. He glanced at me with his watery, pale-blue eyes. They swam fishlike behind his thick glasses. He wiped the back of his hand across his nose again.

"It's fall. October," he replied. I nodded. Killer observation. He nodded too.

God, I felt sorry for the guy. Maybe I was the only person who ever talked to him. Gary took out a stained hand-kerchief and blew his nose.

"Well, don't let me keep you, Gary. That looks like a wicked cold you have there. And you probably have lots of other mail to—"

"Nah, pretty much finished the route. Did it in two hours, twenty-three minutes today."

Yes, he times himself. And has to talk about it.

"Hey, nice. Sweet. One of your better times. Well, I better—"

"You hear about all the break-and-enters in the neighborhood?" Gary said suddenly.

No way. Gary was actually talking about something other than the mail or the weather. My brain snapped from half-asleep to alert.

"Yeah. Mom told us. People on the corner. Two doors down. Across the street. Next street over."

"Yep. Five so far. Couple new ones yesterday. Bet you didn't know *that*." Gary can also be a bit of a jerk. "At 218, the yellow house. And 198. Wait, is it 196 or 198?" He paused to puzzle out this detail. What did I care what the house number was? There had been five—no wait, now *seven*—break-ins in our neighborhood in the past two weeks! That was the important point.

"Yeah, 198," he said with a nod. "That one with the hedge. Lady there was talking to the cops when I delivered." Gary seemed quite cheerful with this neighborhood crime report.

"Jeez."

"Don't worry, kid. Don't worry," he said.

Do I even have to say how much I *hate* it when he calls me "kid"?

"I'm not *worried*," I lied. "The cops will stop—"

"Because," said Gary, cutting me off like I wasn't even speaking, "*I'm* watching. I'm out there. On the ground. Every day. And I'm watching." He pointed two pasty fingers at his thick glasses.

I almost laughed out loud. Detective Gary. Mild-mannered mail carrier by day, fearless sleuth by night. Gary sniffing around for clues. Getting in the police's way, probably. Screwing things up to add some excitement to his dismal life.

"Well, good. That's good, Gary. Those thieves better watch out. But, you know, you should be careful. They might be dangerous."

"I'll be okay. It's *them* that better look out." He looked more ridiculous than ever as he said this. He literally puffed out his chest. Then, mercifully, he turned to leave.

"Go get 'em, Gary," I said. I quickly shut the door, in case he turned around.

As I locked it, I thought about the break-ins. Mom was sure spooked about them. She was leaving on lights all night long. She had got Uncle Dave to trim the bushes near the back door. She would not be happy to hear about two more houses broken into.

Poor Mom. So many worries. About us, about her job, about Uncle Dave. Like she needed this added stress. It made me mad thinking about these jerks, freaking out people like my mom (and, let's face it, *me*).

So much stuff stolen in the neighborhood.

So many houses broken into.

So little being done about it, it seemed. The cops wrote up reports, but Mom said they told the neighbors there wasn't much chance of tracing their stuff. The thieves were pretty smart, the cops said. Only took smaller things. Grab and run. Quick resale. They didn't back up moving trucks and clear out the houses completely.

But now Gary was on the case. I felt a little guilty for wanting to laugh at that. *Gary* at least had the guts to get out there and try to help. What was *I* doing? Nothing.

I was smarter than Gary. Way smarter. Not so socially awkward. Better vision.

I'd watched *Sherlock* on Netflix.

I had nothing to do this whole week other than be Tom's legs. And running up and down the stairs, fetching and carrying, was already getting old.

Maybe I'd do a little detecting of my own.

Chapter Two

"Another package for you," I said, tossing it onto Tom's lap.

"Oh, good. Probably the audio interface." Tom started ripping into the box. "What took you so long?"

"Gary. The guy makes what should be a ten-second delivery into an awkward, ten-minute chat."

Tom grinned. "Is he your new friend, Charlie?" Gary is a legend in our house.

Uncle Dave and Mom hide, literally *hide*, when they see him stumbling up the walk.

"Yeah, right. The guy is *nosy*. Isn't it illegal or something for a mail carrier to ask what's in your mail?" Then, not caring that I was being nosy too, I asked, "How much are you spending on all this stuff?"

"None of your business. Not *tons*. Some of my job money."

Tom works at Sport Shed. *Worked* at Sport Shed. Maybe he will again when he can actually walk around.

"Oh, hey. There's been another couple of break-and-enters in the neighborhood. That's what Gary said. I don't know if we can believe him."

"Really? Jeez. Mom will freak."

"Gary could be making things up for a little drama. A bit of excitement. He's in full crime-fighter mode."

"That's *all* we need," said Tom, laughing.

"Look, you want anything else? Got your medicine? Water? I'm going to go for a walk."

"Nope, I'm good," Tom said. He was studying the instruction manual for the electronic blah-blah he'd just gotten. I grabbed the cereal bowls. One empty, one a soggy mess. Tom looked up. "Thanks, buddy."

"No prob." Tom was, in fact, a really good guy. My best friend, if I wanted to get all emotional about it. So mostly I didn't mind doing stuff for him. I knew he'd do the same for me.

I ran down to the kitchen to unload. I noticed a blinking light on the answering machine.

Hi, this is Carly Silberman from the office at Walter Watts High School. I'm calling about Charlie's absence from school. We'll just need a note to confirm—

I pushed *Delete*. I had told Mom the school was okay with my taking a week off to help Tom.

"That's so good of them!" she had said. "They must know how close you guys are. And you're such a good student, Charlie. Missing a few days shouldn't affect your grades at all."

What I didn't tell Mom was that I had lied. I had been emailing notes about my absences all week as Mom—Gloria Swift.

I wanted to help Mom out. She had been working double shifts lately. She was worried about how Tom was going to manage on his own. Uncle Dave was out all the time "job hunting." There was only me.

Thing is, I desperately needed a break from my new school anyway. I was doing great, grades-wise. I had a much higher average than Tom. But high school isn't only about grades. It's not even mostly about grades. I needed a break from walking the halls alone. From timing my arrival to make sure I got to school right at the bell so I didn't have to stand alone in the hall. From pretending to talk on my cell phone at lunch so nobody thought I was a loser.

Other than us both having dark hair and blue eyes, Tom and I looked very different, that was a fact. He was tall, I was short (but really hoping for a growth spurt). He was athletic, I was not. He was relaxed and easygoing and popular. I was none of those things.

Mom had no idea how miserable my life was. Even if she did, she would say I needed to give it time. To make friends at a new school, to feel more comfortable there. I knew all that. But it didn't make it any easier. And I wasn't about to start worrying her with my problems.

Tom's injury had been the perfect opportunity for me to take a break.

As I stacked the bowls in the dishwasher and wiped down the kitchen counter, I planned my route. I was going to walk past the two houses that just got broken into and see if I could gather any information. Clues. Observations.

Maybe the police needed a bit of help solving these break-ins. An extra pair of eyes. Somebody who knew the neighborhood. Somebody who would blend right in.

Somebody who had no idea what he was getting himself into.

Chapter Three

I stepped out of our house and hung a left.

As I walked, I thought about why someone would decide to become a thief. I mean, did they sit around with their friends, kicking around job options, and settle on *thief*? How did that work?

McDonald's? Nah, not fast food. Too much grease. Grocery store? No way am I wearing those weird aprons.

Hey, I know! How about stealing other people's stuff? Yeah, maybe burglary *is my future*." Seriously. Is that how they made the decision?

I know, I know. They would likely argue that they would make a lot of money with less time and effort by stealing stuff. That is true. No doubt about it. But it's *other people's stuff*. Stuff that other people have spent their money on. But I guess thieves aren't really sitting around worrying about the moral side of their job. Or they wouldn't be thieves, right?

But even if they didn't think it was *wrong* to steal stuff, weren't they afraid of getting caught? You might think this would be a total deal breaker. Break and enter, possession of stolen property—I've seen the crime shows. That gets you into a whole scary world of police and courts and possible jail time. *Jail*. Do thieves actually think they're smarter than the entire police force? That they won't get caught? Seriously? I couldn't imagine getting away with something like that. I can't lie to save my life. (Mom says my ears always turn red.)

I tried to get inside the mind of a thief. Someone completely, totally different than me. I thought of busting a back window or forcing a lock, then slipping into a strange house. Once you get past *Why on earth would they ever do something so wrong?* you come to *I wonder what would that feel like?*

To a thief, stealing probably feels exciting. Maybe nerve-racking. But once they get away with it, they might think how easy it is. They might try to convince themselves that being a criminal isn't so bad. Easy money. Nobody gets hurt. People just buy new stuff. But thieves never seem to think about how it *feels* to have something stolen. Not to the steal*er* but to the steal*ee*.

My family's been pretty lucky so far. I've only ever had my bike stolen. I had left it outside a store. The thieves smashed the lock and took it. They must have been desperate, because it was a piece of junk. Rusted up and murder on the hills. But I wandered around for, like, twenty minutes, confused. I thought I had forgotten where I left it. It was a very weird feeling to discover that something of mine was just gone. But imagine if it was something *inside your own home* that went missing. That would be a terrible, scary feeling. Somebody going through your stuff. Your *mom's* stuff.

When I was in eighth grade, a girl in my class once told us how her house had been burgled. The thieves had dragged a neighbor's ladder over and used it to crawl into an open second-floor window. Full-on robber mode. They'd stolen bikes, jewelry, iPads. The usual kind of stuff you might expect a thief to take. But they'd also taken some left-over pizza from the fridge. *Pizza.* I think that freaked me out most of all. The idea of strange people in your house stealing stuff but also being relaxed enough to have a snack. Taking your family's *food.* Creepy.

I was just passing the yellow house, the one Gary said had been hit the day before. Looked all right to me. No damage to the front door. Nobody around. I walked past it slowly. No smashed window, no police tape. Would they put up police tape? Probably not. Anyway, I didn't see any. All in all, from a crime-show point of view, a big letdown. I even walked down the back lane and peered over the fence at the house. Nothing unusual.

I walked down to the house second from the corner. I was starting to feel kind of stupid. Gary had probably just invented these two latest robberies because he's so excited about this whole thing. There are people who do that. Lie about crimes just to get attention. Or report useless things to the police or pretend to have witnessed something. Gary might be that kind of weird.

The front of the house looked fine. Peaceful, sleepy. But as I was passing, a door at the side of the house opened and a woman stepped out. She jumped a little when she saw me and watched me walk by with her eyes narrowed. I barely looked over, but I could see that the glass in the top half of the door had been smashed. A few strips of duct tape crisscrossed the frame.

I was in business.

There really *had* been a break-in. The jumpy lady and that door proved it.

Okay, so where did that get me? I had to think. I kept walking, down to the park at the end of the street. I sat on a bench. It was a little chilly, so I slipped my hood up.

Seven break-ins (I was willing to believe Gary now). Ten days, maybe two weeks since they had started. In this neighborhood. Why here? This wasn't a rich area. Maybe it was someone who knew the area, who felt comfortable here. Could it be someone who actually *lived* in the neighborhood?

In my head I went over the list of people I know by name or by sight. It is a long list. We have lived in this neighborhood since I was about three years old.

My mind ticked off house after house.

But did we really *know* any of these people? For example, our next-door neighbors. The Brants on one side and old Mr. Lee on the other. We said hi when we saw them. My mom talked to them if she was out raking leaves. Tom and I shoveled Mr. Lee's walk when it snowed. But did we really know them? An image of Mrs. Brant popping in for a quick robbery on her way to the grocery store flashed through my mind. Of Mr. Lee using his walker to smash a window. Ridiculous. Stupid.

Calm down, Charlie. You're freaking yourself out.

I tried to be logical. Realistically, what type of person could be a robber? I left old people and young mothers off my list of suspects. I supposed it was possible in theory for a new mom to park the baby in the backyard, pick a lock, burgle a house and be home in time to pick up the other kids from school. But really? Seriously?

Let's face it—this seemed like a young person's kind of crime. And

I thought it was more likely to be a young-*guy* kind of crime. Why? Well, men tended to commit more crimes than women did, didn't they? Maybe I was being sexist though. Young women could be every bit as talented robbery-wise as young men. I didn't doubt that. So I settled back on just young people.

I was pretty sure about robbery being a young person's crime. Climbing in windows, hauling stuff, stealing pizza, running away…you couldn't have, say, a bad back and be a really effective thief. I added that to my list. So now it was no old people, young moms, children or people with bad backs.

This was starting to feel a little ridiculous.

But Sherlock always said to eliminate the impossible, and whoever is left, no matter how improbable, must be the culprit. Or something like that.

A door opened across the road. At the car guys' house. One of the car guys came out. Tom and I always call them the car guys because we don't know their names. And they always have a bunch of cars parked on the street that they work on. So very witty of us.

Anyway, those two guys were definite possibilities. They were youngish. Maybe mid- to late twenties. Uncle Dave's age maybe. Come to think of it, they had the same kind of jean-jacket, shaggy-haired look as Uncle Dave, only they were both blond. Brothers, we thought. They looked like they wouldn't have any trouble moving quickly, maybe even while carrying heavy stolen objects. They clearly had lots of stuff, including—I squinted to count the cars in the driveway and on the road—one, two, three, possibly four cars. And nobody knew what they did for a living. Suspicious? I sure thought so.

Just then one of them pulled into the driveway. The garage door opened. I sat up straighter. The garage was packed! Stuffed with boxes and bags from floor to ceiling. The car guy got out of the car, opened the trunk and grabbed a box. Then the other car guy helped, carrying more boxes from the trunk into the garage. After that they closed the garage door.

I started to get excited with this new possibility.

See? Just a little quiet thought, and sometimes you could—

Wait. Somebody else was coming out of the house. A guy in a hoodie. He stopped to say something to the others, then walked away quickly. He was carrying a couple of heavy-looking bags.

I got up and crossed the park, slipping from tree to tree. I was trying to stay hidden as I followed. Okay, the guy was walking away from me, but still. That's the kind of thing you do when you do detective work. You stay out of sight.

He was a big guy. Hood up. Baggy sweats. He seemed a bit familiar somehow, but he wasn't one of the car guys. There was something about that back. That shambling walk.

He turned to check for cars at the crosswalk, and I got a glimpse of his face.

Unbelievable.

I was following Uncle Dave.

Chapter Four

Uncle Dave! I almost laughed out loud. I had been so caught up in being stealthy that I hadn't recognized my own uncle.

I started to run to catch up with him, but then I stopped. The more I thought about the situation, the more strange it became.

Fact: Uncle Dave was broke. He had lost his job as an appliance-repair guy.

That's why he had moved in with our family a couple of months back.

"Uncle Dave's going through a bit of a rough patch," Mom had said. "But you guys will love having him around. He's such a sweetie. A big heart." Mom had a soft spot for her little brother. He was paying rent, I knew. But not much.

Fact: Uncle Dave had lots of time on his hands. He *said* he was at the library, updating his résumé, job hunting. But was he really? Or was he breaking into people's houses and stealing their stuff?

Fact: I had *seen* Uncle Dave coming out of the car guys' house. And by my very scientific process of elimination, I had already determined that they were the most likely suspects for the break-ins. Was he friends with them? Was he part of their gang? Or maybe he didn't do the stealing. Maybe he was the one who sold the stuff. A partner. An accomplice.

Fact: Uncle Dave was young(ish) and fit(ish). He would have no trouble climbing through a window or breaking the lock on a door. He was strong. He'd carried Tom up to our room like he was a ten-year-old.

Fact: Uncle Dave had been acting strange lately. He stayed out late most nights of the week. He had stored a ton of boxes in the basement. *God.* All those boxes! Why had I never thought twice about all those boxes? I had assumed it was just his stuff from his old apartment. But I remembered him saying something once about his things being in storage. So what was in all those boxes? He'd better not be using our house to store stolen goods.

Fact: Our house hadn't been targeted. Why not? Because Uncle Dave wouldn't do that to his own family? I mean, good. Thanks, Uncle Dave, but still…

There were a lot of strikes against good old Uncle Dave.

I picked up my pace.

Now he was right in front of me, skulking along the street. Hauling those heavy, heavy bags. His head was down, like he was thinking.

Yeah, I hope you're thinking about how you're going to explain going to jail to your sister and her kids.

"Hi, Uncle Dave," I said. Very casual. Not at all suspicious.

"Charlie! Dude, you surprised me there," he said. He looked nervous. "What are you doing?"

"Oh, I'm just out for a walk. Want me to help you with those bags? They look heavy."

Uncle Dave pulled the bags closer to him.

"Nah, thanks. I got 'em. We're almost home anyway."

"So what have *you* been doing, Uncle Dave?"

"Not much, not much. Met up with a friend for coffee. Library. Job hunting. The usual."

Riiiight. Job hunting at the car guys' place. This was going to kill Mom.

When we got home, Uncle Dave bolted downstairs. Was it my imagination, or was he acting guilty? Or was he just being his usual slightly awkward Uncle Dave?

"Hi, Tom! We're home," I called up the stairs. "Dinner soon."

"Great. I'm starving!" he yelled back.

I went into the kitchen to fix dinner. My specialty: frozen pizza and pre-peeled baby carrots.

I wondered whether I should talk to Tom about Uncle Dave. But what did I actually know? So far I had no real proof.

Tom is nicer than I am. He'd explain all my so-called facts about Uncle Dave away so they'd look more ridiculous than suspicious.

No, I decided to keep it to myself for the time being.

I'd wait until Uncle Dave went out that night. He went out almost every night. Volunteer work, he would say. Or meeting a buddy for beer. Upgrading his online job-hunting profile at the library. Hitting the gym. It was always something. Mom said it was good that he was getting out, that it was healthy.

But what if, instead of stacking cans at the food bank, he was casing houses to rob? What if he was pawning stolen property at one of those seedy shops downtown?

Not so healthy, Mom, I thought. Not so healthy.

I'd wait until he was out of the house, and then I would go down and check some of those boxes in the basement. That was my plan. It was the sort of no-brainer thing any detective would do.

And not feel guilty about doing it.

Chapter Five

"Well, thanks for the pizza, Charlie," said Uncle Dave, scraping some crusts into the compost bin. I'll say this for Uncle Dave—he does help with the dishes.

"Hey, I made it myself, just for you."

He laughed. "Well, I better get going. Helping out at the food bank tonight at the warehouse."

"Wow, again?" I said. "You must be

their hardest-working volunteer."

"Nah, but I try to get there a couple of times a week. You and Tom going to be okay? Your mom is working another double shift, right?"

"We'll be fine." I watched him stack the dishwasher. "So you really like volunteering there?"

He looked surprised. I guess I'd never shown much interest before.

"Yeah, I do. Good people, you know? Very friendly crowd. You should come sometime, check it out."

That was unexpected. A thief wouldn't invite somebody to check out a fake volunteer job, would they? *Unless* they were very, very clever. Throwing people off the scent.

"Maybe I will, thanks." *We'll see, Uncle Dave, we'll see.*

Uncle Dave glanced at the clock. "Well, I'd better head out. Sure you guys will be okay?"

"Yeah, don't worry. See ya, Uncle Dave."

"Have fun, little buddy." He pulled on his jacket and shouted, "Bye, Tom!" before he left.

I let a full ten minutes go by. Just in case he'd forgotten something. Just in case he came back. But he didn't.

The basement was all mine.

Let's be honest. It wasn't the best part of the house. Dim lights, ratty old carpet, a dusty treadmill. A pull-out couch was opened into a bed with rumpled blankets. A TV on top of some Ikea drawers completed our "luxury bachelor suite."

That's what Mom calls it.

"Let's let Dave have the basement. It can be his bachelor suite," she'd said when he moved in. She had been so excited. He was her only brother, younger than her by eight years or something like that. They are pretty close,

I think. Anyway, it was good for Mom. Another adult to talk to, someone in the house when Tom and I went to visit Dad. Though that wasn't happening so much lately, with his new girlfriend in the picture. Fine by me.

So it would really, really suck if Uncle Dave turned out to be the jerk robbing everyone in the neighborhood. It would be a betrayal of a lot of things. A betrayal of Mom. I really hoped my suspicions didn't turn out to be true.

I went over to the boxes stacked against the wall. There were a lot of them, maybe ten or fifteen. Some open, some still sealed up. I got to work.

First box: books. Certainly not stolen. Or if they were, Uncle Dave was one weird thief.

Box under that: some old dishes. Nope. The stuff looked like it came from a thrift store.

Next box: vinyl records.

Box after that: hockey cards.

Box after box after box. I went through them all. There was lots of stuff. Candlesticks, vases wrapped in paper, wooden bowls, a bunch of framed pictures. And then I opened a small wooden box. Jewelry. *Jewelry!* A whole box of it.

My heart sank. I should have been excited. Triumphant.

But I wasn't. Because I realized that what I was doing down here was trying to prove to myself that Uncle Dave *wasn't* the thief. And now I was looking at a box of jewelry he had stashed.

"Shit," I muttered, closing it back up. The dishes, the records, the hockey cards, the books…all of that was probably his. But jewelry?

I knew nothing about jewelry. What was valuable, what was not. All of this stuff looked shiny and sparkly. Some of it looked old. Where the hell had he gotten it? *Why* did he have it? Could there possibly be another explanation?

A little voice inside me said, *Nope.*

I checked through the other boxes. More stuff. Random stuff. Confusing stuff. Horseshoes, an old lady's brush-and-comb set in engraved silver, magazines from the 1980s, toys. Toys. What the hell would Uncle Dave be doing with toys?

I closed the last box. I felt completely baffled. So much weird, random stuff. No iPhones, electronics, watches or money. But that box of jewelry haunted me.

I stood up and stretched my back. It was killing me from bending over so long. My eyes fell on the two bags I'd seen Uncle Dave carrying away from the car guys' house. I unzipped the first one. Speakers. A microphone. Cords. In the second bag was a keyboard, some pedals, more cords.

"Shit," I muttered again. Because this seemed to clinch it. This was expensive, portable stuff. And I'd never once heard Uncle Dave play an instrument.

I had to talk to him.

I had to find out why he was doing this.

I had to get him to *stop*.

Chapter Six

"You're quiet," said Tom. "Weirdly quiet."

"Just tired, I guess." And worried. So very, very worried.

We were lying on our beds in our room. We'd put bookshelves down the middle so we could each have a little privacy, but we could still talk to each other.

"I'm trying to figure out how the hell to connect this thing to the keyboard," Tom said. "What are you doing?"

I'm trying to figure out how the hell to save Uncle Dave from going to jail. But I wasn't going to tell Tom anything until I'd talked to Uncle Dave. I thought maybe if I could just make him see sense, if I could get him to somehow turn over the stuff, maybe we wouldn't even have to involve Mom.

"Nothing. Just lying here."

"Well, do something. Read a book. Watch a show. Hey, *I* know! *Spy*. Maybe we'll catch those thieves. Want to play a round?"

Spy is a game we have been playing since we were young. It is simple. Basically it involves each of us looking out the window with our binoculars and seeing what we can see. That's it. Sounds lame, I know, maybe even creepy. But it isn't. Nothing much ever goes on, so the point of the game is to take very regular, boring things and make them sound funny or ridiculous.

From our room, we can only see the sides of some houses, patches of street, backyards. Sometimes one of us used to go into Mom's room, spy out her window and report loudly on what we saw.

"Yeah, sure. Unless this is just for pity. Sympathy-spy," I said.

Tom laughed. "Nah, this thing is pissing me off, and I'm tired. I'll look out our window, and you look out Mom's."

"So, full-spy?"

"Okay." Full-spy is where we do a running commentary of what we are seeing, trying to make it funny. For example, a full-spy of the Greys' house might go: "Mrs. Grey is at nine o'clock…garbage bag in each hand… wait…she stumbles…drops bags… we can only imagine the foul-mouthed swearing!" Mrs. Grey runs a day care and is the sweetest lady you'll ever meet.

We've almost never seen anything important. Nobody interesting lives near us. But that was the funny part. We made it seem like the innocent people around us were total maniacs.

I clicked off the lights and went and stood at Mom's window.

"O'Donnells are watching TV," called Tom from our bedroom. "*Breaking Bad*...scanning for meth lab in their basement..."

"Mrs. Sharma scrubbing windows," I called back. "Must have been a lot of spattering from that knife attack..."

Maybe you had to grow up with the game to appreciate it.

Anyway, we kept it up for a while. My binoculars swung left to right, house to house, back and forth.

Tom was calling out something about the new guy who lived down the way smoking in his backyard. But I wasn't listening.

Because I had just seen something that made me pause. The house two doors down from the one behind us was totally dark. But there was a little flitting, flickering light upstairs. I could only see it once in a while. It danced along the windows at the back of the house, sometimes stopping, sometimes moving on.

I opened my mouth to play-by-play to Tom. Then I closed it.

That was a flashlight. A little one, but it was definitely a flashlight. Who uses a flashlight in their own home? Nobody. Nobody unless there is a power outage. I flicked Mom's bedside light on and off. No outage.

I ran to our bedroom.

"Tom, Tom, I think the thief is in *there*. In *that house*," I stammered, pointing out our window. But we couldn't see it very well from this angle. What I didn't say was *And I think the thief is Uncle Dave.*

"What? What makes you think that? Did you see them?"

"I saw a flashlight—it was a pretty small one, but it was all over the place."

"Well, that doesn't mean it's a *thief.* I mean, we've used flashlights in here."

"Yeah, but…"

I made a quick decision.

"I'm just going to go over there for a second. Just to see."

"I don't know if that's a good idea, Charlie. I can't help you." Tom pointed to his cast. "What if things go south?"

"I'm not going to do anything stupid. I'll just see what I can see. That's all. It's, like, three houses away. You can even watch me with the binoculars.

There's a bit of an angle where you'll be able to see me. Anyway, I'll just have a quick look."

"Okay, but promise me you're not going to do anything else. No being the hero. Mom would kill me if you got killed."

"Promise. I'll be careful. It's probably nothing anyway. I'll be back soon."

I pulled on my hoodie, slipped on my shoes and went out through the back door. Straight through the backyard. Over the fence. Through the O'Donnells' backyard, up to the sidewalk. Then left one house, two houses.

Uncle Dave, if that's you in that house, I swear to God I am going to lose it. You will have one hell of a freak-out on your hands, buddy.

The house was completely dark other than the porch light. I slipped behind some bushes and watched the upstairs

53

windows. Nothing. No flickering light. Had I just imagined it?

I inched closer to the front windows. All the blinds were down, but one had got caught up on the corner. There was a small triangle of uncovered window.

I moved closer to the triangle, as close as I dared, and looked in.

I saw the thin beam of light on the main floor. Sweeping from side to side. Dancing up out of my vision, then coming back down. I was breathing hard now, my heart pounding. At one point the thief was right on the other side of the window from me. The little beam of light dropped to the floor, falling on the thief's running shoe. I could actually make out that it was black with a smear of white paint or something on the toe.

I only saw it for a split second before a rumbling sound made me jump. What *was* that? Car headlights swept down the street, and I realized the garage door was opening. The people who lived here were coming home! Which probably meant the thief was going to come flying out of the house. But where? Back? Side? *Which* side?

I was desperate for a glimpse of him. I'd know Uncle Dave's shape, even if he took off at a run, wouldn't I? I heard a scrambling at the back of the house. The sound of feet running, bushes snapping. It was so dark, so confusing. The hum of the garage-door opener made it hard to pick up other sounds. I ran to the corner of the house and collided with somebody. Hard.

The person lashed out at me.

"Get him! *Get him*! What the— *Charlie*? Is that you? Did you see the guy?"

The guy grabbing me was Gary. Gary the mail carrier, grabbing my arms, shaking me. We stared at each other in the gloom, panting. He looked past me, his eyes getting huge behind his glasses.

"He's getting away!" he whimpered. "Where…? *There! There* he goes! Down the alley!"

I whipped around and looked toward the alley. I thought I saw a movement over there, a shadow out of the corner of my eye.

We ran to the mouth of the alley. I beat Gary there by, like, five minutes. Let's just say his skills are not those of an athlete. I looked down the alley. Dead still. And dark.

Was the guy long gone? Or was he crouched there in the dark, hiding behind a garbage can? That was a seriously creepy thought. Who knew? And I wasn't about to find out.

"Uncle Dave?" I whispered. Just in case he was there. Just so he knew I knew.

Gary pounded up loudly, finally catching up to me.

He was really struggling to catch his breath. "I almost…had him. So…close." He started coughing, bending over, the coughs racking his skinny body.

"Take it easy there, Gary. Have you been out here *looking* for this guy?"

"Patrolling," he said through his coughing. Then he got it under control. "I've been watching out as often as I can. I was so close tonight. So close! I saw the flashlight! I would have shown that thief who's boss. *I* would have shown him."

Gary, what on earth would you have done if you caught him?

I had never felt so sorry for him. Lurking around in the dark, night after night, hoping tonight would be his big chance to be a hero.

But then again, *I* was lurking around in the dark too. But that was different somehow.

"I'm sure you would have, Gary. Look, did you *see* the guy? Anything?"

"No. Just the flashlight," he said dully. His shoulders sagged. "You?"

"Not much. Pretty much nothing. Just the beam of the flashlight. I was going for a walk. Thought I'd check it out."

"Shoot." Gary took off his glasses and wiped his face with a handkerchief. His eyes looked moist and red. "I saw a shadow run out of the house," he said. "That's it. A shadow. It seemed tall. Fast."

To Gary, almost anyone would be tall, but my heart sank.

Uncle Dave was pretty tall. I'd never seen him run though. Was he fast?

And where the hell was he now? That's what I wanted to know.

Chapter Seven

When I got home, Tom wanted all the details. He hadn't seen much (you couldn't from that window), but in a gap between the houses, he said, he had seen some guys running. I tried to give him a good story—me out there in the dark, practically catching criminals with my bare hands, blah, blah, blah. I didn't mention my suspicions of Uncle Dave at all. But that almost felt like lying.

I wasn't used to hiding things from Tom.

Mom came home around eleven. She looked tired and worn out. I sat with her in the kitchen for a few minutes while she ate some yogurt.

"You okay, Charlie?" she asked. "You're pretty quiet. What did you and Tom get up to today?"

"Nothing much. Spy game."

"You guys still play that?" She laughed, shaking her head. "I really appreciate that you've been taking such great care of Tom. What would we do without you, Charlie?"

"No prob. We're fine, Mom. Don't worry about us."

She yawned. "Man, that was a killer of a double shift. But I'll be home early tomorrow. Tom's got that appointment with the surgeon at four thirty. Why don't you come with us, and then we'll get burgers after?"

"Sure, yeah, sounds good." I was barely listening. What I was listening for was the door. I needed to talk to Uncle Dave. Tonight. I'd never get to sleep if I didn't.

I might not get to sleep if I did.

"So tired," said Mom. "I'm heading up. Love you, baby." She kissed the top of my head. "You should get to bed soon."

"I will. I just have to…I have to do this thing for school." Lie. Ears turning red.

I sat in the dark living room, waiting for Uncle Dave. That's what they always did in the movies when someone was going to confront somebody else. They sat in the darkness and *waited*. The time ticked by. Eleven thirty. Eleven forty-five.

Footsteps on the path up to the front door. A thud. A rattle of keys. Then the door opened.

Uncle Dave came in, kicked off his shoes, bent over and then neatly set them to the side. Would a criminal type actually do that? I mean, it was a little thing, but sometimes little things matter. Tidying up your shoes shows respect for other people, right? I was desperate to find any excuse for him. I liked him. I'd always thought he was a good guy. *Was* he a good guy?

I had to find out.

He was heading to the stairs. "Uncle Dave!" I called out.

He jumped big-time. I flicked on the light.

"Jeez, Charlie, you scared the *hell* out of me! What are you doing sitting there in the dark?"

"Actually, I'm waiting for you."

"Why? Is everything okay? Is something wrong?" Again, this concern for other people. It was nice to see. It made me doubt my suspicion.

"Everything's okay. I just need to ask you some questions."

"Okay…like, now? It's pretty late. Could it wait—"

"It can't wait."

He came and sat down on a chair. He looked completely puzzled.

"Where were you this evening?" I shot the question out at him.

He frowned. "At the food bank. The warehouse. I told you. Why?"

"You can't have been there until now."

"Well, no. Look, Charlie, what *is* all this?"

"Uncle Dave, I've been thinking about all the robberies in the neighborhood—"

"Doing some detecting? Good for you! Found anything out?"

I looked at him closely. He seemed interested. But not in a guilty way. Just regular interest. He was relaxed. Loose.

Time to go in for the kill. I just hoped this didn't get ugly.

"That box of jewelry you have downstairs. Where did you get it?"

"Jewelry?" He looked confused. His eyebrows went up.

"In the boxes against the wall downstairs."

Uncle Dave's eyebrows relaxed. "Oh, *that*," he said. "I got that from… wait a second, you went through my stuff?"

"Well, yes. Sorry. There's a lot of stuff down there, right? And I thought, I thought…" It was pretty hard to say it right out loud. *I thought you might be the thief.* So he said it for me.

"You thought that I might be the *thief*!" He said it with a shout of laughter. "*Me*?" He clapped a hand to his chest, laughing. Then he saw that I wasn't laughing.

"Charlie, hand to God, I've never

stolen a thing in my life. Not one thing. Not a chocolate bar, not a...not a grape from the grocery store!"

"Everybody steals a grape once or twice. They let you."

"Mmm, maybe. But you probably shouldn't."

This was not going how I thought it would go.

"The jewelry," I stammered. That was a fact. "Also bags of musical equipment."

Uncle Dave ran a hand through his hair.

"Look, Charlie," he said with a sigh, "the job market's so tight, I thought I'd start a side hustle. That's what they call it. Some work you do on the side, you know? Only right now it's my main hustle. Anyway, I've got a little business going. I've been buying stuff at thrift stores and garage sales and reselling it on eBay."

I must have looked skeptical, because he rushed on. "It's true. I'm getting pretty good at it. I got that little jewelry box *full* for five bucks, and I think there's a brooch in there worth at least thirty. Old. Vintage. I even pull stuff out of the garbage. Free! It's amazing what people throw out. Found a pair of snowshoes last week. Got forty bucks for them! Pure profit. I figure out when garbage day is for the ritzy areas, and I look around. They're throwing the stuff out—it's not stealing."

He looked down at his hands.

"Maybe that's embarrassing to hear. I'm sorry if it is." Uncle Dave sat back and ran his hands through his hair again. "I didn't tell you and Tom about it because maybe *I'm* embarrassed by it. But it's honest money, Charlie. I told your mom. And I'm making more now, so I can chip in a bit more for living here."

"Well, that's good," I said. I felt really bad for ever suspecting him. "Look, Uncle Dave, I'm really sorry for going through your stuff—"

Uncle Dave held up his hand. "Stop. Forget it. You were just trying to figure things out. Come to think of it, it probably *did* look pretty suspicious!" He put his hand over his mouth because he was laughing. "Look, I'll come clean. Totally clean."

I leaned forward. What was he going to confess to?

"The music equipment isn't for my business. I'm in a band, dude! I always *wanted* to be in a band. Played piano as a kid, so I'm on keyboard. It's with the guys down the street, the ones who work on their cars all the time? Good guys."

"The car guys? Down the street?" The guys who had just become my main suspects now that Uncle Dave seemed to be in the clear? Those guys? "I don't know. They look pretty rough."

"They're cool," Uncle Dave said. "Josh and Kyle. Drums, guitar. We practice almost every evening. I love it, man."

"Tonight? Did you practice tonight?" I said quickly. Just because Uncle Dave was in the clear didn't mean my detective work was done.

"No, they couldn't. I went on a garbage run after the food bank. Glendale is a gold mine. Found a side table. Teak! Solid wood and needs oil, but I bet I can get fifty, sixty bucks for it! I left it on the porch. Do you want to see it?" He started to get to his feet.

"Maybe tomorrow. Look, Uncle Dave. How well do you know those car guys? Josh and Kyle. Like, have you been friends for a long time?"

"Not super well, I guess. Couple of months. Just got talking one day about one of their cars. Anyway, they said they needed another guy for their band. Got a space set up in their basement. I thought we might practice in the garage, but it's crammed with stuff."

Yes, all that stuff in the car guys' garage.

Guys Uncle Dave has only known for a couple of months.

Guys who seemed to have lots of money for cars and musical equipment.

I had some work to do.

Chapter Eight

"Doorbell," said Tom. As usual he didn't even look up from his computer.

"Yeah, I heard it," I said blearily. I looked at my clock: 9:00 AM. I put my pillow over my head.

The doorbell rang again.

"I think it's probably Gary with another package," Tom said. "Sorry," he added when he saw my face. "It might be my midi keyboard."

The doorbell rang *again*.

"Oh my god," I said. "Can't he just leave the package on the porch?"

"With people stealing stuff all over the neighborhood? Please, Charlie. Could you just get the door? I owe you one."

"You owe me *lots* more than one. Like, maybe…*twenty*." I'm not very witty when I'm tired.

I ran down the stairs and checked the peephole. Gary. Of course.

"Hey, Gary."

"Hi, Charlie. Another package for ya. For Tom, actually."

"Thanks." I grabbed at it, but he held on.

"Another Amazon. Music Central."

I ground my teeth together. Again with the prying.

"Yep," I said.

He let go and took out his handkerchief. He swabbed his runny nose.

The poor guy had probably caught a cold with all his nighttime patrolling. He kept standing there, like he wanted to say something else. As usual, I didn't have the heart to close the door on him.

"Hey, kid, those thieves didn't get anything at that house. I asked the cops. I talk to the cops a lot."

I'm sure they're real *happy about that, Gary.*

"So no need for you to go poking around. Me and the cops, we got it covered. Bad luck last night. But I'm on it." He looked at the mailbox as he said this.

Despite all the bragging and lumping himself in with the cops, Gary actually seemed worried about me. I was touched.

"Well, okay—"

"Could be dangerous. You never know," Gary said to the doorbell.

"Anything you're not telling me, Gary?" I asked.

"Nah. Well, nothing you need to know." He smiled a little at a bush. "Nothing you need to know."

Okay, I was sick of these sneaky attempts to get me to keep talking. I needed to get rid of him.

"You're right, Gary. You are absolutely right. I'll leave it to the *professionals*." The sarcasm went right over his head. "You be careful out there."

"I will, I will. I got it covered."

An alarming thought popped into my mind. Gary wouldn't actually have gotten himself a gun for his night patrols. He wouldn't be that stupid. Would he? Was he the kind of guy who might do something like that? *Dangerous*, that's what he'd said. That was a scary word. Did he mean the thieves, or what he'd do to them if he caught them?

"Look, don't do anything stupid, okay?" I called after him.

He wasn't even listening. He'd turned around and was halfway down the path, his bag banging against his thin little legs.

Great. Just great. I already had Uncle Dave to worry about. He had promised to look in the car guys' garage next time they had band practice. *Just to prove there's nothing there*, he said. To prove to me they were good guys.

But what if they weren't, and they found him there, snooping around their stash of stolen stuff? So I was worried about that.

And now I had Gary to worry about too.

Chapter Nine

It took Tom what seemed like three years to crutch downstairs and out to the car for his doctor's appointment. I tried to get him to slide down the banister. Both practical *and* fun, I argued. Mom didn't think it was such a great idea.

"We don't need *another* broken leg, Charlie," she said. Fair enough.

Turns out, we didn't need to hurry after all.

"Dr. Washington is running *at least* forty-five minutes late," said the dead-eyed clerk at the desk. No "sorry." No explanation. She may as well have added, *So just sit down and suck it up*.

"Okaaaaay," Mom said with a sigh. "So we could just wait here, or we could go get burgers *now*, instead of after the appointment. Anybody hungry?"

Tom and I were pretty much always hungry. And let's be honest—I was only along for the burgers anyway. Sitting in the doctor's office reading ancient *Sports Illustrated* magazines was not my idea of fun.

So we went and grabbed an early dinner. The burgers were great, and not only because Tom and I had been living on cereal and frozen pizza. Mom told us stories from the operating room.

She was funniest when she was mimicking the doctors. It was nice to see her relaxed and happy.

And the bonus: now she wouldn't have the extra worry that her brother was a criminal. Because now I knew he wasn't. So all good.

We went back to the doctor's office and settled down to wait.

"Hey, Mom," I said, "do I have to stay or is it okay if I just walk home? It'll only take me about half an hour. I wouldn't mind getting some exercise." There was no reason for me to be there. Now that the burgers were eaten.

"Sure," she said. "Got your phone? Text me when you get home. Dave's probably going to be out, just so you know."

I knew. Tonight was when he was planning to go to the car guys' house to snoop around for me. I'd made him promise to ask some questions. Have a peek in the garage, if he could manage it. He had said he'd try.

But I was definitely feeling a bit nervous about Uncle Dave doing any kind of detective work. He just seemed too *obvious*, somehow. Too honest. I still couldn't believe he'd never eaten a grocery-store grape.

"Charlie, don't do anything stupid, okay?" Tom whispered as I passed by. I'd said exactly the same thing to Gary. That was good advice. For Gary. This was insulting.

"I won't, I won't." I'd filled Tom in on everything. He knew we were now focusing on the car guys and their stuffed garage.

It was getting dark as I walked home. Even though I told myself to think about other things, my thoughts kept turning to the break-ins. To the thieves. I didn't have a whole lot else going on in my life, to be honest.

I passed by the car guys' house. I could see that the lights were on in the basement. And I could hear the heavy beat of the drums. Band practice was on. Uncle Dave was in the house.

Don't do anything stupid, okay, Uncle Dave?

I kept walking until I reached our house.

If I were a thief, I thought as I approached our front door, how would I break into *this* house? Never through the front door. There was no cover at all. It was a straight walk up from the street, and there was a very bright porch light. No bushes, nowhere to hide. No, if I were a thief, I wouldn't chance being seen from the street. I'd head around back.

So I headed around back. This was more like it. It was really quite dark at the side of the house. But problem time: there was only way in, and it was the dining room window. It was high off the ground. Like, small-ladder high. And I doubted the thieves were carting around ladders, big or small. I thought they would look for an easier way in.

I moved on. I went through the gate to the backyard. Mom had the porch light on here too. But because of the trees, the back door was way more private. It was a definite possibility. I pictured a tall shadow lurking at that door, picking the lock, slipping inside...

I stumbled to the door and reached for the doorknob, suddenly afraid. Locked. Thank goodness. I felt weak with relief. My imagination was *way* too active.

Okay, Charlie, settle down. House is all locked up. Stop freaking yourself out. You are so pathetic...

I took out my key and let myself in, slipping in as silently as the thief I imagined. I locked the door quickly behind me. Safe. *When did I get so jumpy?* My nerves felt stretched to the limit. I took a couple of deep breaths and bent to untie my shoes.

Thud.

What was that? I froze. A dull *thud*. Upstairs.

I straightened up very slowly. I strained my ears to hear.

A dull thud. I swore I had heard a dull thud. Like something falling on the carpet. *Did I actually hear that, or did I imagine it?* I stood still, trying to hear over the loud pounding of my heart.

Nothing. I listened again. Nope, nothing.

I shook my head at myself. Wow, I was so *tense*.

I relaxed my shoulders (which had clenched up somewhere near my ears). Did a little back stretch. I was just reaching for the light when I heard the floorboard outside our bedroom creak.

I snapped to attention. It felt like my heart actually stopped or missed a beat or something. I was that scared.

There was no explaining *that* sound away. I knew that one. And I had heard it as clear as day.

It's a family joke, that floorboard. Tom and I had named it Creaky McCreaker (we were, like, four and seven at the time). It was just put in wrong or something. Uncle Dave had tried to fix it a while back, and now it creaked even worse. You had to step *over* it if you wanted to avoid the creak.

Everyone knew that. Everyone who lived in this house.

So the person upstairs was somebody who didn't know you had to step over Creaky McCreaker. Somebody who didn't even know it was *called* Creaky McCreaker. Somebody who didn't live in this house.

A stranger.

A thief.

A thief-stranger was upstairs in our house.

Chapter Ten

The thought that there might be someone in my house made me almost dizzy with fear. The house suddenly seemed a strange and sinister place. A scary place.

There was dead silence now. Listening silence. Like that loud creak had frightened the person upstairs too, and they had frozen. So now there were two of us in the house who were frozen, listening.

I felt very vulnerable standing there in the back entrance. I moved a small step back into the coats that were hanging on the hooks. The faint smell of my mom's perfume wafted from one of them. I sunk deeper.

I groped silently around me for some kind of protection. I pawed at backpacks, gym bags, coats, scarves. Did we own nothing *hard*? Nothing *sharp*? My hand closed on an umbrella. That was at least something I could swing. It would have to do.

I didn't dare move. I didn't dare try to leave. I hardly dared to breathe. I just stood in the dark back entrance, listening. I felt for my phone in my pocket. Not to call 9-1-1 because I didn't want to have to whisper and blow my cover. Who knew what these thieves would do if they heard me?

Tom. I'd text Tom. I shielded my phone with a coat and quickly typed.

thief in house come now

I felt a little better. Less helpless.

Until I heard the person upstairs moving again.

What could I do? What could I possibly do? Rush up there with an umbrella? Scream the place down? Actually, I considered screaming. Making a racket might scare them away. I wanted to scare them away without them hurting me. I wanted to make them *leave*. Basically, I wanted some cops with megaphones and whistles to appear.

Wait. *Whistles*. Tom's gym bag was on the floor beside me. Tom had been a camp leader at a soccer camp this past summer. A leader at a soccer camp probably had a whistle! I inched open the zipper on the bag and shoved my arm inside. While I felt around in there, I listened to the person upstairs.

Slight, stealthy sounds. Footsteps.

My hand scrambled over things in the gym bag, identifying them by feel—cleats, socks, shin guards, card, cord. *Cord.* I gently pulled on the cord, gathering it into my hand a little bit at a time. Was this a whistle or just a shoelace? It seemed like the longest shoelace in the whole world. But just when I was going to give up, I came to the end of the cord.

And I felt the whistle.

I pulled my arm out of the bag and put the whistle to my lips. I paused.

I still had a choice. Should I hide here and stay safe, or should I scare the living hell out of whoever was upstairs trying to steal our stuff?

I surprised myself by picking option number two. I took a deep breath and blew.

The shrill blast of the whistle ripped into the silence. I heard an immediate flurry of activity from upstairs as I sucked in a quick breath. I blew again, the sound unbelievably loud and weird in a dark, still house.

The advantage of a whistle is that it's hard to pinpoint. It's just a wall of sound. It could be coming from anywhere. I kept blowing on that whistle like my life depended on it. Maybe it did.

The thief must have flown down the stairs, because he was on the main level in a heartbeat. The guy was fast, fast, fast. I saw a shadow bolt from the bottom of the stairs into the kitchen as I blew another blast. I saw a dark form against the white kitchen cabinets, and then, slippery as an eel, the guy slithered out the kitchen window.

I kept blowing on that whistle for a few more seconds just in case the guy had any friends still rummaging around somewhere. I stopped and listened for a long minute. Nope. Nothing but silence.

I raced over to the window and slammed it down. I tried to lock it, but the lock had been broken. Forced.

I ran down the hall to the front door to make sure it was locked. Because I hadn't actually checked that. Because all of a sudden I felt very, very vulnerable.

But as I ran down the hall, I heard a familiar sound. Dear lord, the front door was *opening*.

I stopped dead. I might have even whimpered. And I blew and shrieked on that whistle again, very, very hard.

"Charlie, *Charlie!* Buddy, it's me, Uncle Dave!" He flicked on the hall light and ran toward me. His eyes were full of concern. "Are you okay? You okay?"

"What the *hell* are you doing coming in here like that?" I screamed at him, punching him on the shoulder.

Okay, that was unfair. The man lives here. I was a little tense.

"What? Me? I got a text from Tom saying there was a thief in the house! So I dropped everything and rushed home. You okay? What the hell is going on?"

"Robber. Thief. Upstairs. Out the window." I was shaking pretty bad by this point. And having problems speaking in full sentences, apparently.

"Is he still here, do you think?" asked Uncle Dave, clearly looking around for some kind of weapon.

"No he's not still *here*!" I said, like he should have known that. "I scared him off with the *whistle*. I don't think he took anything, but I'm not sure."

"Jeez Louise." Uncle Dave turned and locked the door. "Good job, little buddy. So he's gone? Like, for sure, for sure?"

"Fired out through the kitchen window. I saw him go."

"You're sure you saw him leave? And there was only one of them?"

Uncle Dave looked uncertainly up the stairs. Up the dark stairs. "Well, I guess we better check—"

Poor Uncle Dave. He looked as freaked out as I felt. How had I ever thought he could have been the thief?

He cleared his throat. "All right. I'm going to go check that everything's okay up there."

"Yeah, you go check," I said. "Here." I handed him the whistle and the umbrella. "Just in case."

He flicked on the hall light and climbed the stairs.

"Holy *hell*," he exclaimed from the top of the staircase.

"What, *what*?"

"Well, let's just say you saved your brother a whole lot of money," he said. He turned and held up two gym bags brimming with electronic equipment.

"Uncle Dave?" I said. My voice was a little unsteady, which was really annoying. "Were both car guys at your band rehearsal?"

He stared down at me.

"Only Josh was," he said slowly. "Kyle said he had something else to do."

Chapter Eleven

"Doorbell," said Tom, the next morning.

"Oh. My. *God*," I said, rolling my eyes. "I can't face another conversation with Gary. I really can't, Tom." We'd been up late, giving a statement to the police. I'd asked them if they were close to getting these guys. The tired-looking cop just shrugged his shoulders and kept filling out his forms.

"It's the last package. DJ controller." Tom looked at my face. "Okay, forget it. Maybe he'll come back later."

The doorbell rang three more times. I could not believe how persistent that little freak was. Four rings. Wasn't that excessive? Wasn't that practically harassment? There it went again. Five rings. Six.

"This is ridiculous," I muttered. I slammed out of the room, ran down the stairs and wrenched open the door.

Gary jumped like he hadn't been expecting me.

"Oh, hi. Thought you guys might not be home."

"So you rang the doorbell many, *many* times. Sorry—took me a while to get down here." I held out my hand for the package. But Gary had a firm grip on it. How sad was it to hold some-one's mail hostage to get them to talk to you?

"Any news about the break-ins?" he asked.

"As a matter of fact," I said in a snotty tone, "we had a break-in *here*. Last night. Didn't see *you* patrolling the frickin' neighborhood, *Gary*."

"*Here*? Like, this *house*? Oh man." He sounded so disappointed. "When? I was patrolling over past the park."

"They got away. Didn't get anything though."

"Good! Listen, I've been watching that house across the park. The one where those two guys work on all those cars."

"Really?" I was surprised. Somehow Gary had come to the same conclusion I had. This made me feel uncomfortable. It made me want to rethink everything. "You got any proof?"

"I'm working on it." He smiled and nodded at the potted plant on the step. "Your uncle is there a lot."

"Uncle Dave's a good guy, Gary. He is not involved, so you can forget about him. Better yet, leave the investigating to the cops, Gary. Just leave it."

He handed me the package with a scowl and made his way back down the steps.

The talk with Gary left me unsettled. There was a niggling little something in the back of my mind that was worrying me. I felt like I'd noticed something over the past few days that might have been a clue. What was it? And why did talking to Gary remind me of it? Because he'd mentioned the car guys' house? What was it about those car guys and their house?

Everything kept coming back to them.

Chapter Twelve

Tom had taken his pain medicine and was fast asleep, even though it was only early afternoon. It really sucked for him to be in so much pain. The doctor had said his leg was healing well but that there was still a long way to go.

The doorbell rang. Tom wasn't even awake to point it out.

Who on earth could that be? We had already had a call from our number-one visitor today. Probably somebody selling something. Or maybe Uncle Dave had forgotten his key. He'd gone out hours earlier. Band practice. I guess when nobody had real jobs, they could practice whenever they wanted.

"Have you looked in their garage?" I'd asked when I saw him leaving.

"I'm working up to it, okay? You can't just rummage in somebody's garage with no excuse. I'd look like a fool if they caught me at it. But I really don't think Josh and Kyle are your guys, Charlie. Or Amanda."

"Who the hell is Amanda?" I demanded. Was this someone I needed to add to the suspect list?

Uncle Dave looked surprised.

"Their sister. You've never seen her? She lives there too now. Just moved in a few weeks ago. She's super cool, so nothing suspicious there." Uncle Dave's face was getting a little pink. Oh, great, now there was romance clouding his judgment.

"Look, Uncle Dave, just try to get into that garage." It was the last thing I said to him before he left.

The doorbell rang again.

I closed my book, ran down the stairs and peeked through the peephole.

Unbelievable. It was Gary again. It was truly depressing that *Gary* was the only visitor this house seemed to get. We seemed to be the guy's personal project. I looked at his little head in his big ballcap and sighed. Then I opened the door.

"Hi, Gary," I said dully. I stopped myself from saying, *What do you want?* I went for something a bit more polite. "Another package? You don't usually deliver this late."

"No, no, no package." Gary looked nervous. Agitated. "Look, I have talk to you," he said to the ground. "It's about the break-ins. I found out something. And I just have to talk to *some*body." He put a trembling hand up to his damp forehead.

"Well, okay, but—"

"—because I have proof! *Proof*." He looked over his shoulder. Before I even knew what was happening, he'd pushed past me and shut the door. He looked back through the peephole. "I feel like I'm being *followed*," he muttered.

"I really doubt that, Gary."

I tried hard not to find all this drama kind of sad. And annoying. But I was curious. He obviously had something. Or thought he had. What if he'd actually stumbled upon a clue? Some actual evidence?

"Well, pull up a chair," I said sarcastically. He had already collapsed into a chair and dumped his bag down on the floor. I sat across from him on the couch.

"Is Dave around? Maybe I can talk to him."

"Nope. It'll have to be me," I said briskly. I was determined to keep this short and sweet. "So what's this proof you have?"

He leaned back in his chair and wiped his forehead with that putrid handkerchief again. "You got a glass of water?"

I ground my teeth and went to get him a glass of water. Everybody's servant—that was me.

But as I handed him the glass, a strange thing happened.

"Thanks, kid," he said to his shoes.

I glanced down at his shoes. They were dirty. My first thought was, I hope he doesn't stain the carpet with those dirty shoes.

Those shoes…those shoes were familiar. I looked closer.

And then something in my mind clicked. The shoes I was looking at, the ones on Gary's feet, were black. Black shoes. But on the left one, there was a splash of white paint on the toe. I saw it clear as day.

As clear as the day I had seen it in the beam of a flashlight. A flashlight inside that house the night Tom and I had played Spy. The night Gary and I had chased the thief.

That was the niggling thing I'd noticed. The thing that had been bugging me. It was seeing that black shoe with the splash of white paint. Spotlighted in that house by the flashlight. Neighborhood break-in number seven. Or eight. I couldn't remember.

I hadn't thought the shoe was important at the time, but it *was*.

Lots of people have black shoes, I argued with myself. *Many people paint things.* But I knew I was right. It was the same shoe. The same paint splash, one that looked like a big comma. It was a clue. It was the shoe of the thief. The shoe of Gary. Gary's shoe.

Gary, who had told me to back off investigating the break-ins because things might get dangerous.

Gary, who was sitting right here. Alone with me. Tom was upstairs, asleep. Even if he wasn't, what could he do? Throw a crutch?

My mouth got dry. My heart started to pound.

Suddenly, Gary looked straight at me. Not at the carpet, not at the couch, right at me. Right into my eyes. The bumbling, sickly mail guy was gone. The pale blue eyes were alert. Intelligent. Amused. *Dancing*. A giant smile spread over his face, showing crooked, yellowish teeth.

"So tell me, kid," he said, "was it you with the whistle?"

My blood ran cold. I hadn't told him how I had scared off the thief. The only way he could have known about the whistle was if he was the other person who'd heard it. The only other person in the house. The guy upstairs, trying to steal Tom's stuff.

At that moment I knew for certain that he was the thief. And as we looked at each other, I knew that *he* knew that *I* knew.

"It was, wasn't it?" He chuckled. "Not bad, not bad. Rattled me, I admit. A whistle has a *cop* feel to it somehow. Man, I slid down that banister quick, like a ten-year-old! I wish you could've seen me. Just a shame I couldn't finish the job. That's some choice stuff your brother has up there. Would have been a big haul."

"So it was you," I croaked.

Gary laughed then, throwing back his hair with a flip of his tiny head.

"He finally gets it! Give the boy a prize! Took you long enough. Ah, you should've seen your face just now!" He laughed delightedly and wagged a finger at me. "You were all supposed to be out. You and your mom and your brother all went *out*. I saw you. And that loser uncle of yours left just after that."

A flame of anger shot through me. *Don't call my uncle a loser. At least he's not a little rat of a thief like you. And how dare you spy on my family, track our movements and break into our house?*

"I came back early."

"Exactly. You came back early. Big mistake."

He was clearly enjoying this so much. Having the time of his life.

"Not really," I said. "Got rid of you, didn't I?"

Gary's smile faded. "Admit it. When you heard me upstairs, you were scared stiff. Just admit it. That must have been nerve-racking, hey? Was it?"

I wasn't going to give him the sick satisfaction of agreeing with him. He knew. He just had some twisted need to hear me say it.

"You think you're so smart, kid," he sneered when I refused to answer. "You're *smug*, you know that? You're just a sniveling little loser like your uncle. I'll tell you who's smarter than you. Me, that's who! I've been stealing stuff for months. All over the city! Never got caught, not even close. Cops don't have a goddamn clue."

He watched my face. He settled back in his chair, stretching out his legs. Like he owned the place.

"And then you came along. Little Charlie. What are you, twelve, thirteen?"

"Fifteen," I said. Seriously? Twelve? Even in the midst of stress and panic, I was offended.

"Really? You look way younger. Anyway, you come along, thinking you'll do some detecting. Thinking you know better than the cops even. Don't make me laugh. You literally *ran into a thief* the night I came flying out of that house. You didn't suspect me for a second, did you? I did a good job there, didn't I? Improvised on the spot! *Did you see him, did you get him*?" Gary mimicked the panicky questions he had fired at me that night. "When it was me all along! I should be an actor, that's what I should be. Pulled that one off like a total pro. I just about died laughing seeing you sprint down that alley to catch the imaginary thief! I had to fake a coughing fit to cover laughing my *ass* off."

He laughed again. His laugh sounded like a horse whinnying. It was seriously irritating.

"Ahhh, good times," he said, clearly not done talking yet. He took off his glasses and wiped his eyes. "Don't you have anything to say, kid? Nothing?"

I shook my head. He seemed disappointed.

"Come on, don't be a bad sport! You got outsmarted. Humiliated even. Deal with it." Gary shrugged his shoulders and started laughing again.

My lack of response seemed to annoy him. He stopped laughing. He tilted his head and looked at me for a minute. Those watery eyes were sharp. Alive. Angry. And let me tell you, serious Gary was *way* scarier than laughing Gary.

He leaned forward, his elbows on his knees. He pushed his face near mine.

"I've never liked you, kid. Never. Always answering the door with that bored face. Always making such a big show of being *so* nice to poor Gary. Such a loser, that Gary. Poor, stupid, boring, sick, pathetic Gary. That's what you thought, don't deny it. Well, let me tell you, I ain't poor now. I'm rolling in cash. I cleared $7,000 this month alone! Who's the loser now, Charlie?"

My turn to stare him down.

"Why are you telling me all this?"

"Because I *want* to. It's just so *sweet* telling you all about it! I've been so smart that I need somebody to *know* about it! That's half the fun. Half the fun," he repeated, leaning back in his chair.

You're still pathetic, Gary. You may not think so, but you are.

"I also like the actual stealing," he said. Like we were having some kind of normal conversation. Talking about what kind of ice cream we liked. "Stealing's a huge thrill. Not just regular shoplifting. Done that, but where's the fun in it? It's over so quick. Houses. That's what I like. Wandering around other people's houses, seeing what they got, imagining them freaking out when they find that things are missing. It's *power*. And I'm getting good at it, so damn *good* at it. I got it down to a science. You know, I even hit a house twice. Twice! After they'd replaced the stuff I stole the first time! Suckers."

I was starting to shake. This whole thing seemed like a very bad dream. The kind of dream you have where people you know are strangers. This was a stranger sitting in front of me. This was no skinny, sad mail carrier. This was a criminal, through and through. A warped, angry and bitter person. One who got his kicks from robbing other people.

"So what's to stop me from going to the police?" The question just slipped out of me. Had I really thought about it, I might not have asked it. I hoped the answer wouldn't be him pulling a gun on me.

He seemed delighted by the question.

"I was hoping you'd ask that!" He laughed, throwing his hands up in the air. "And the answer is: *nothing*! Go tell the cops every last word. See? That's the beauty of it. You can't touch me even if you talked! You've got no proof."

He didn't know I'd seen his shoe that night. Was that proof? Was it enough?

"You've got a story nobody in their right mind would believe," he continued. "Gary? The thief? That runty little mailman with the sniveling cold? Don't make me laugh. Even if the cops checked out my place, they wouldn't find anything. Like I'd keep anything there. No, Charlie, everyone would assume you're some pathetic loser kid trying to get his name in the papers."

He was right. He was absolutely right, and he knew it. He looked at me with a kind of laughing pity. *Gary*, pitying *me*.

"So now you're going to know it's me and *keep* knowing it's me when you hear about *more* break-ins," he said. "Just watch me. Track my career. You've got lots of time. You're just a kid. You think you're so smart, but you're just a kid. And remember, nobody would believe you. Your own mother wouldn't believe you. Nobody!"

"I'd believe him," said a loud voice from somewhere down the hall.

Chapter Thirteen

"Uncle Dave!" I had never, ever been so glad to see anybody in my whole life. *Ever.*

Gary leaped to his feet.

"Charlie and I were just having a little chat," he muttered as he slipped his bag over his shoulder. He was back to being stumbling, pathetic Gary. He even took out his handkerchief and blew his nose. But the eyes looking at Uncle Dave were very sharp.

"How much did you hear?" I asked Uncle Dave. "Did you hear him admit that he's the thief? That he's the one doing the break-ins? He bragged about it." I wished my voice didn't sound so shaky and shrill.

Gary looked completely confused and innocent. "What are you talking about?" He turned back to Uncle Dave. "The kid's crazy. Watching too much *Sherlock*. Get a life."

"Get the *hell* out of here. Now!" snarled Uncle Dave. He lunged at Gary. Uncle Dave was way bigger than him, but Gary moved lightning quick. He slithered over the back of the couch, yanked open the door and sprinted down the walkway.

I heard him laughing that whinnying laugh as he ran.

"He's getting away, he's getting away!" I screamed. "We have to go after him!"

"No way, Charlie. I think we'll leave that to the police." Uncle Dave locked the front door and collapsed into the chair Gary had been sitting in moments before. "We'd never catch him anyway." He was smiling.

"Are you *kidding*? We have to do something! He just confessed everything to me! Everything! He's the thief, Uncle Dave. Do you understand? You believe me, don't you? *Gary* is the thief. Oh man, is he actually going to get *away* with this?"

"Nope," Uncle Dave said calmly. He took a little silver box out of his pocket and held it up for me to see.

"What the—what is that?"

"Tape recorder. Old school. Five bucks at a garage sale. I use it to record band practice, so I can see how I sound. If I'm improving."

"Um, well, congrats. Neat gadget. Look, have you even been listening to a word I've said?"

"Of course I have!" Uncle Dave sounded hurt. "I came in the back door, like, ten minutes ago. Slipped in while that little weasel was laughing his head off. I've been following him since yesterday, when I saw him going into the pawnshop a few doors down from the thrift shop. He was carrying a big, heavy bag."

I looked at Uncle Dave with new respect.

"Did you go in, talk to the—"

"Of *course* I did. Just chatted up the owner of the pawnshop while I looked around at the music equipment. Told him I recognized the guy that just left. Turns out he's a *very* regular customer."

"Well, that's great, Uncle Dave." I was trying to be kind. But the owner of a pawnshop might not be the best witness we could've hoped for. "I guess we have to take his word for some of it."

"But that's just it, Charlie! Once I thought about it, Gary seemed more and more likely to be our guy. He knows the neighborhood. He is always around. He knows individual *houses*. He probably delivers half the stuff he steals! And when I saw him coming into our house as I was walking home from practice, I didn't know what he was up to. But I knew it wasn't good."

Understatement of the year.

"No, it wasn't good, Uncle Dave." I said. Suddenly I felt very tired.

"Anyway, now we have *Gary's* word for everything!" said Uncle Dave, laughing.

I must have looked confused. He pointed at his recorder.

"Uncle Dave," I whispered, "did you actually—"

"Yep. I heard him bragging about the break-ins, so I snuck down the hall and recorded your conversation! He incriminated himself pretty good, I'd say. You did an awesome job of stringing him along, Charlie, making him talk!"

So being scared and silent was good for something.

"Heh-heh, yeah. I sure let him talk."

Uncle Dave pressed a button on the little machine. There was a whirring sound. He pressed another button. Gary's mocking voice floated into the room as clear as day: "*Man I slid down that banister quick, like a ten-year-old.*"

"Yep, got the whole thing."

We grinned at each other.

"High five, Uncle Dave," I said.

Chapter Fourteen

"Wow, that little *shit*," said Tom that night as we lay in our room in the dark. "Had us all fooled. Well, *almost* all of us."

"Not Uncle Dave," I said. I was still impressed with him.

"Well, right, but I was talking about *you*! You spotted the shoe. You knew he was the thief before he even opened his mouth. Didn't you?"

"Yeah," I said truthfully. "Yeah, I guess I did. Everything just clicked into place when I saw that shoe."

Uncle Dave and I had run upstairs and played the conversation for Tom (who was choked to have missed all the action). Then we called the police. They came to the house a little while later, and I wrote out a statement. Don't mean to brag, and I know it's pretty cool, but that's what I did. The police seemed interested. *Very* interested.

So did Mom. She didn't freak at all. She thought it was all pretty logical— a sad, frustrated person trying to get a bit of power and excitement in his life. She was just glad nobody got hurt.

The police called later to say Gary had been "apprehended." It still seems weird to think about Gary as this master thief, as a person who might be heading to jail.

A reporter from the city newspaper also came by to interview me and Uncle Dave. He said he was going to call the story "Neighborhood Watchdogs Catch a Thief." Which is a pretty catchy title, I think.

"What a weird few days," Tom said.

"Yeah." I yawned. I had to go back to school this week. But the thought of that didn't rattle me as much as it had before. I felt calmer about everything. Uncle Dave was going to help Tom out this week and get some tips from him about making electronic music. There were no band rehearsals because the car guys were away, helping their folks move into a condo. They'd stored a lot of their parents' stuff in their garage. I know, I know. I was *so* wrong about them.

I was wrong about a lot of things. I am no detective, really. But I do have a *very* active imagination. This whole thing has made me think about writing stories.

Mysteries, maybe. I think I'd be good at those.

"Charlie? You asleep?" Tom called out in the dark.

"Obviously not."

"Spy?" he asked. I could almost hear his smile.

"Sure!" We grabbed our binoculars.

"Car guy on the street at ten o'clock," I whispered. "Walking with a girl. Car *girl*."

"Owl. Two o'clock!"

"Old guy walking a little dog…stopping, sniffing…moving on."

We were quiet for a long time, scanning the neighborhood. It was a good neighborhood. Safe. Quiet. Lots of big trees. People who knew each other. We'd grown up here.

"Nothing much happening." Tom yawned.

"Nah. But that's kind of how I like it," I said.

Acknowledgments

Thanks to Tanya Trafford, a skilled editor who actually makes edits enjoyable, and to the team at Orca Book Publishers for their commitment to reluctant readers. I'd also like to acknowledge the generous support of the Alberta Foundation for the Arts for this project.

Alison Hughes is an award-winning author of many books for children and young adults, including *Hide and Shriek* in the Orca Soundings collection. Alison gives frequent presentations at schools, libraries and young-writer conferences. She lives in Edmonton.

9781459818736 PB

Chapter One

The others can't decide if it's better to hide or to be "It."

They've argued about it, tossed around pros and cons. On the one hand, hiding's more fun, more creative. But on the other hand, It has the power. It is the hunter.

Hiding is definitely more my style. I'm little, for one thing. And quiet.

I can stay very still, not moving a muscle. You should hear the others when It gets blindfolded, shouts, "Go!" and starts the countdown. Crashing all over the place, banging into things, thumping down the alley. Like a herd of elephants. Honestly, if you're It and you just *listen*, you can pretty much figure out exactly where they all go. That's what I do when I'm It. Listen.

But when I'm hiding, I use the other hiders' noise as cover. Part of my strategy. You can slip in anywhere if you're quiet and careful. And here's a tip. The very best hiding spot is within a few feet of the person who's It. I know it sounds crazy. But it's not. That spot is pure gold. But you have to hide while they're still counting—*during* the count, from one to maybe thirty, while the others are making their finding-hiding-spots noise.

It takes guts. There's a whole count from thirty to one hundred, seventy double beats, when the noise of the others has died away. By then you have to have found your hiding spot and stay absolutely still. That's when you actually *hear* your heartbeat whooshing. And your breathing sounds way too loud. You start telling yourself that It will rip off that blindfold, look you right in the eye and the game will be over. But so far, so good. The strategy hasn't failed me yet.

I shake it up, of course. I mean, you can't hide right near It every single time. Obviously. And even though my sister, Tess, says it's practically cheating, it's not. It's not against the rules.

The only rules of our hide-and-seek club are:

1. No leaving the yards or the back alley on our street
2. No going inside
3. No breaking into anywhere or locking gates behind you

4. No moving spots once you've hidden
5. No cheating on the count to one hundred
6. No cell phones

We don't play the kind of hide-and-seek where you have to race whoever's It back to home base when they find you. All that yelling "Home free!" and the wild sprinting, the scuffling, the collisions—that's all for children. I'm glad *we* don't play that way. It is undignified for teenagers. Plus, Tess, Cam and Dylan would outrun me every time.

Our game is based on skill, not just speed.

Tess is still annoyed about that one time I lay against the bottom of the fence she was leaning on. The fence was home base, and she was blindfolded and counting to one hundred. I crawled in while the boys were sprinting down the alley. And I stretched out right in front of her, practically at her feet. My only cover was a few long, prickly weeds. I turned my face to the fence and waited. That was a gamble. *That* one tested my nerve. I wouldn't have done it with Cam or Dylan. I don't know them so well.

But I've watched Tess be It so many times. I've watched her for years. She follows a pattern. She's impatient. She does the count leaning against the fence, like most of us do. We usually start in the same spot, at the fence right by the Reillys' garage. I don't know why we picked that spot, but it's where the game always starts.

When Tess does the count, she gets more and more restless as it goes on. She hates having to be still. She can't *wait* to hunt. She's a natural It. Like Cam. Both action people. Runners. They suck at hiding, by the way.

By eighty, eighty-five, you can see she's just *dying* to seek. At ninety-five she's already turning away from the fence. At ninety-eight she's grabbing the bandanna. And at one hundred she yells, "Ready or not, here I come!" She yanks off the bandanna, tosses it aside and starts running.

Anyway, that one time, Tess never saw me lying there right at her feet. She turned and ran, exactly like I predicted, looking to either side of her. But never *behind* her. I was the last one found, lying there in the alley right where she started, against the fence, right out in the open. The hide-and-seek club, all four of us, laughed a lot at that one. Well, it took Tess a little while to laugh. First she whined about the spot being unfair, against the rules, just plain stupid. But she joined in eventually.

I think that might have been the day when everyone started to respect me as a full member of the club. Maybe that's when they saw me as *me*, Emily, not just as Tess's little sister, the fourteen-year-old (almost fifteen) in a group of sixteen-year-olds.

They already knew I was small and freakishly flexible. They knew I could hide in places they never could. Some of the places have become legendary in the hide-and-seek club. The spare tire. The potato sack. The window well. The overturned wheelbarrow.

What they didn't know was that I also have guts.

Good thing too.

I was going to need them.

orca soundings

For more information on all the books
in the Orca Soundings series, please visit
orcabook.com.